WHERE'S THE
DINOSAUR
POO?

ORCHARD

ORCHARD BOOKS

First published in Great Britain in 2020

by The Watts Publishing Group

9 10 8

© 2020 The Watts Publishing Group Limited

Illustrations by Dynamo Limited

Additional images © Shutterstock

A CIP catalogue record for this book is available from the British Library

ISBN 978 1 40836 233 4

Printed and bound in China

MIX
Paper from
responsible sources
FSC® C169965
www.fsc.org

Orchard Books
An imprint of Hachette Children's Group
Part of The Watts Publishing Group Limited
Carmelite House
50 Victoria Embankment
London EC4Y 0DZ

An Hachette UK Company
www.hachette.co.uk
www.hachettechildrens.co.uk

WHERE'S THE
DINOSAUR
POO?

THE MOST TERROR-IFIC POOS YOU'VE EVER SEEN

The dinosaur poos are causing havoc!
From rainforests to supermarkets,
pirate ships to football matches,
they're having a roar-some time.

Can you spot each of the
poos in every scene?

See if you can spot the T-Rex
in one of the scenes, too!

STEGGY

the Stegosaurus Poo
is super-smart and is
always coming up with
cool ideas and
inventions.

ROCKY

the T-Rex Poo is the
coolest in the gang.
He may look fierce,
but he's actually a
bit of a softie.

DIPPY
the Diplodocus Poo is the joker of the group and always pulls silly stunts to make his poo friends roar with laughter!
TRIXIE
the Triceratops Poo is the leader of the group. She keeps all the other poos in check.
RUDY
is the baby of the group. She may look cute but when she's hungry, she gets very angry!
REX
is a roar-some Tyrannosaurus rex. Can you spot him in one of the scenes?

DINOSAURLAND

Welcome to the poos' natural habitat. Can you find them hiding behind the dinosaurs? Ready, steady, go!

UNDERWATER

Splash! The poos have gone for a swim. Can you find them all in this undersea scene?

STEGOSAURUS STAMPEDE

Uh oh, the poos are stuck in a Stegosaurus stampede! Try to find them before they get squashed.

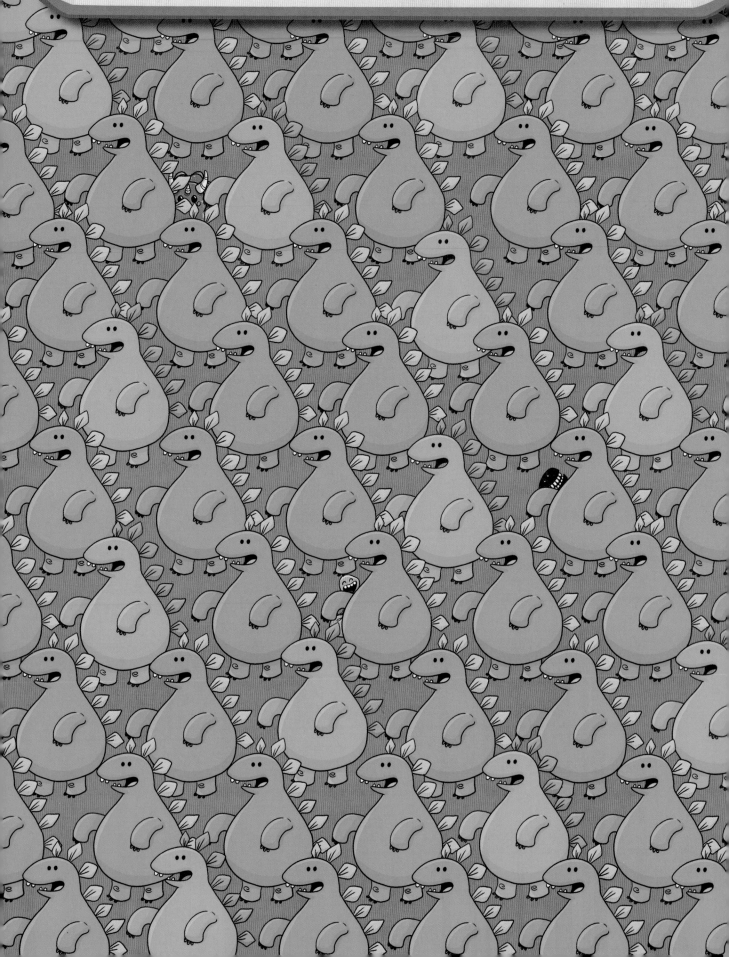

ODD ONE OUT!

Can you find the Stegosaurus that looks different to the others?

MUSEUM

The dinosaur poos have been let loose at the museum. Find them quickly before they make a mess of the exhibition.

SUPERMARKET

The dinosaur poos have popped to the shops. Dippy is looking for lettuce but has got a bit lost. Can you find him, and all the other poos?

Diplodocus Dance

Look at all the dancing Diplodocuses. They had better be careful not to step on any of the dinosaur poos!

ODD ONE OUT!

One of these Diplodocuses is different! Can spot which one?

TREASURE HUNT

Yo-ho-ho! These pirates are used to bad smells, but nothing as stinky as the dinosaur poos. Can you find them all on their latest adventure?

RACE-TRACK

Vroom! The dinosaur poos are getting up to no good at the race-track. Find them before the race is over.

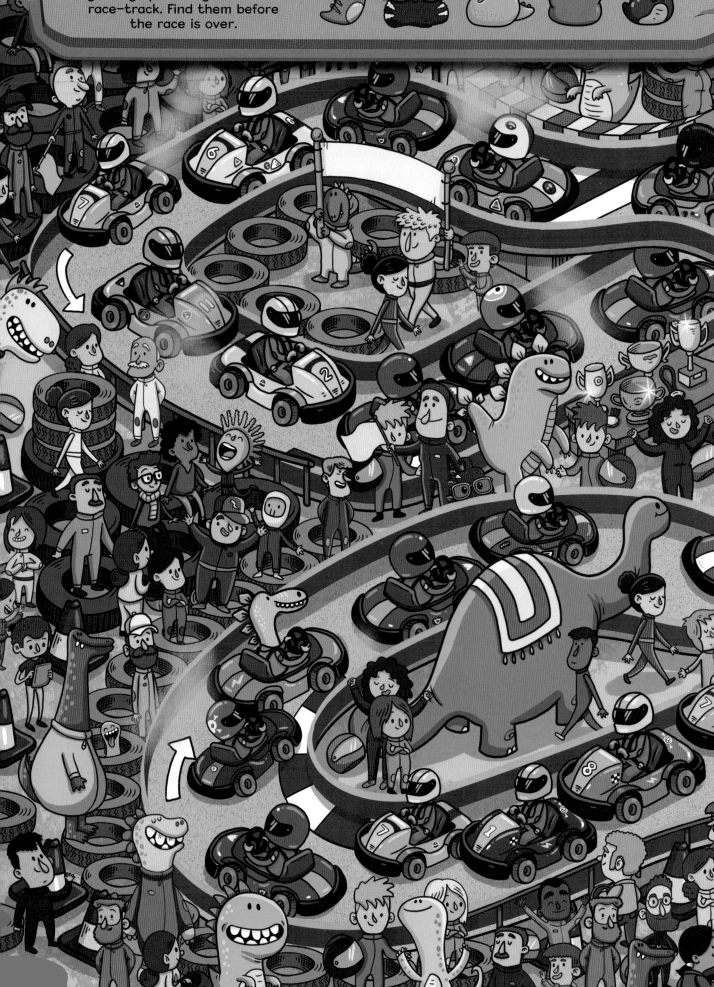

DINOSAUR JUMBLE

The poos are making lots of new dinosaur friends! What's your favourite type of dinosaur?

ICE AGE

Brrrr! Even Rocky the cool poo is chilly out on the ice. Can you spot all the poos before they freeze?

RAINFOREST

Trixie loves exploring in the rainforest! Can you spot her and all her dinosaur poo friends hiding amongst the trees?

Herbivore Mayhem

Dippy the veggie poo is hiding among his herbivore friends. Can you find him? See if you can spot the other poos, too!

ODD ONE OUT!

One of these vegetarian dinosaurs is not quite like the others. Can you spot it?

ON THE MOON

Did you know that dinosaur poos are lighter on the moon than they are on earth? Catch them before they float away!

FOOTBALL

Steggy loves football! His favourite team is Clawsome United. Can you spot Steggy and his friends cheering for the teams in this exciting match?

ANSWERS

Now try and find these
extra items in each scene!

DINOSAURLAND

Two meteors ☐

An old man in a yellow vest ☐

Two women holding wheels ☐

Eight pink crabs ☐

Five skulls ☐

Two fires ☐

Two purple dinosaur eggs ☐

A red T-Rex ☐

Three dinosaurs wearing
tortoise costumes ☐

A blue Triceratops ☐

UNDERWATER

Six grey anglerfish ☐

One red coral ☐

Three pink shells ☐

Four green squid ☐

Four grey eels ☐

Eleven pufferfish ☐

A green fish with pink spots ☐

Eleven pink jellyfish ☐

Seven rocks ☐

Six fish with blue and white stripes ☐

STEGOSAURUS STAMPEDE

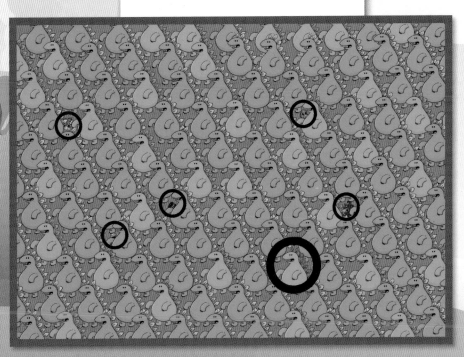

MUSEUM

Nine gold coins ☐

Six mice ☐

A child wearing an eye patch ☐

A man wearing a pink hat ☐

Two men with green hair ☐

A boy with a spider on his shirt ☐

A woman wearing a blue headscarf ☐

A diamond ring ☐

A baby in a pram ☐

A man wearing stripy trousers ☐

SUPERMARKET

A dinosaur wearing a top hat ☐

A pineapple ☐

Two men with lightning bolts on their T-shirts ☐

Three American footballs ☐

Eleven shopping trolleys ☐

Three bananas ☐

Four shopping baskets ☐

Ten brown shopping bags ☐

A boy with blue hair ☐

Three women wearing glasses ☐

DIPLODOCUS DANCE

TREASURE HUNT

A treasure map ☐

Fourteen starfish ☐

Two monkeys ☐

Five periscopes ☐

A pearl necklace ☐

A torch ☐

A surfboard ☐

Four barrels ☐

Seven floating bottles ☐

Two crabs ☐

RACE-TRACK

Four trophies ☐

Two red flags ☐

A podium ☐

Three green flags ☐

Seventeen traffic cones ☐

Two yellow helmets ☐

One green and purple carpet ☐

Four white arrows ☐

A red dinosaur ☐

A yellow flag ☐

DINOSAUR JUMBLE

ICE AGE

Five starfish ☐

Two squid ☐

A red handkerchief ☐

Four eagles ☐

A bear in a blue hat ☐

Two polar bears wearing glasses ☐

Six wolves ☐

Four blue eels ☐

Seven armadillos ☐

Four squirrels holding acorns ☐

RAINFOREST

- Nine spiders ☐
- Nine tigers ☐
- Eight green snakes ☐
- Four flamingos ☐
- Five frogs ☐
- Six toucans ☐
- Four sloths ☐
- Four red snakes ☐
- Eight pairs of binoculars ☐
- Four leopards ☐

HERBIVORE MAYHEM

ON THE MOON

Two telescopes ☐

Nine monkeys ☐

A yellow flag ☐

A woman with pink hair ☐

Four rockets ☐

Two cats ☐

A green cap ☐

Six shooting stars ☐

A pink alien with a yellow stripe ☐

A green alien wearing sunglasses ☐

FOOTBALL

Eight red foam fingers ☐

A dinosaur with a microphone ☐

Two dinosaurs with injured legs ☐

A man in a red and white striped shirt ☐

Five pies ☐

Two Diplodocuses wearing hats ☐

A pair of white boots ☐

Four dinosaurs wearing blue trainers ☐

A referee ☐

A dinosaur flying a plane ☐